CAMPING
FOR FUN!

By Jana Voelke Studelska

Content Adviser: Teresa Rodriguez, Senior Manager of National Partnerships,
National Recreation and Park Association, Ashburn, Virginia
Reading Adviser: Frances J. Bonacci, Ed.D., Reading Specialist, Cambridge, Massachusetts

Compass Point Books ✦ Minneapolis, Minnesota

Compass Point Books
3109 West 50th Street, #115
Minneapolis, MN 55410

Photographs ©: Ariel Skelley/Corbis, cover (left), 21; Germany Feng/Shutterstock, cover (right), back cover; Lars Schneider/Aurora/Getty Images, 4; BananaStock/Jupiter Images, 5; H. Armstrong Roberts/Retrofile/Getty Images, 6–7; Imagno/Getty Images, 7 (bottom); Titus/Stock Image/Jupiter Images, 8; Stephen Mallon/Taxi/Getty Images, 9; Byron W. Moore/Shutterstock, 10 (top); Jakub Cejpek/Shutterstock, 10 (bottom); Konstantin Tavrov/Shutterstock, 11 (top); Hannah Gleghorn/Shutterstock, 11 (upper middle); Kimberly Hall/Shutterstock, 11 (middle); ASP/Shutterstock, 11 (lower middle); Galyna Andrushko/Shutterstock, 11 (bottom); PatitucciPhoto/Aurora/Getty Images, 12 (bottom); Macduff Everton/The Image Bank/Getty Images, 12–13; Peter Frischmuth/Peter Arnold, Inc., 14; Craig Hansen/Shutterstock, 15; Danny Warren/Shutterstock, 16; Martin Sundberg/UpperCut Images/Getty Images, 17; Ron Hilton/Shutterstock, 18; Ulrike Hammerich/Shutterstock, 19; Digital Vision/Alamy, 22; Melissa Garrett/Shutterstock, 23; Sebastian Czapnik/Dreamstime, 24; Ghislain & Marie David de Lossy/Iconica/Getty Images, 25; Anthony Marsland/Stone+/Getty Images, 26–27; Diego Barucco/Shutterstock, 27 (back); Sharon Hay/Shutterstock, 28–29 (top); Olga Lyubkina/Shutterstock, 28–29 (bottom); Mark R/Shutterstock, 30; George Peters/iStockphoto, 31; Royalty-Free/Corbis/Jupiter Images, 32; Ben Blankenburg/iStockphoto, 33 (left); Don Klumpp/Photographer's Choice/Getty Images, 33 (right); Hulton Archive/Getty Images, 34; Sandee Schumacher/America 24-7/Getty Images, 35; David Nielsam/Shutterstock, 36–37; Thinkstock/Jupiter Images, 37 (top); Robert Fullerton/Shutterstock, 39; Shutterstock, 40, 47; Andy Politz/Mallory & Irvine/Getty Images, 41; Library of Congress, 42 (left); Robynrg/Shutterstock, 42 (right); William A. Bake/Corbis, 43 (top left); Jim Harrington/iStockphoto, 43 (bottom left); China Photos/Getty Images, 43 (right); Jhaz Photography/Shutterstock, 44; Runk/Schoenberger/Alamy, 45 (left); John Czenke/Shutterstock, 45 (right).

Editor: Brenda Haugen
Page Production: Ashlee Schultz
Photo Researcher: Eric Gohl
Creative Director: Keith Griffin
Editorial Director: Nick Healy
Managing Editor: Catherine Neitge

Library of Congress Cataloging-in-Publication Data
Studelska, Jana Voelke.
  Camping for fun! / by Jana Voelke Studelska ; content adviser, Teresa Rodriguez ;
reading adviser, Frances J. Bonacci.
     p. cm. — (For fun)
  Includes index.
  ISBN 978-0-7565-3399-1 (library binding)
1. Camping—Juvenile literature. I. Title. II. Series.
  GV191.7.S88 2008
  796.54—dc22   2007032688

Visit Compass Point Books on the Internet at www.compasspointbooks.com
or e-mail your request to custserv@compasspointbooks.com

Table of Contents

The Basics

Doing It

People, Places, and Fun

Note: In this book, there are two kinds of vocabulary words. Camping Words to Know are words specific to camping. They are defined on page 46. Other Words to Know are helpful words that aren't related only to camping. They are defined on page 47.

The Great Outdoors

The fire is burning low, and the marshmallows have been roasted. Your camping buddies are beginning to yawn. The stars are amazingly bright. The air has cooled off after a hot, sunny day. The woods behind you make noises as a night breeze tickles the leaves. You can't wait to snuggle into your sleeping bag. In the morning, it'll be pancakes on the griddle and a day of swimming and fishing. Life just doesn't get any better!

If you've never been camping, it's time to round up some gear and pick a weekend for

your first adventure. If you're already an experienced camper, it's time to plan your next trip. Maybe this time you can check out that campground with the great fishing creek!

The good thing about camping is that it's easy to do. If you don't own a sleeping bag, you can go camping with stuff from your home. Even if you don't have an adult who wants to go with you, you can set up your campsite right in your own backyard.

Camping in Time

Humans come from a long line of campers. Our ancestors camped as they hunted and traveled. Maybe that's why it feels so good to spend a few nights in the outdoors.

Pioneers traveling in wagon trains camped outside for months. Soldiers at war camped on the battlefield. Many Native Americans spent their lifetimes camping. Cowboys on the open range camped. Hotels and inns were expensive and not always easy to find.

When automobiles became popular in the early 1900s, camping took on a whole new twist. It was called gypsying or autocamping.

With food, blankets, tents, clothes, and whatever else they could fit into their cars, people headed out to the countryside. They would find a pleasant spot along a lake, on a mountainside, or in a pasture and set up camp. Magazines and newspapers

printed pictures of families camping alongside America's new roads and enjoying the outdoors.

People liked camping then for the same reasons we like it now. It's less expensive than a hotel or resort, and the pace is slower. Trains and planes have schedules to keep. At fancy restaurants, you have to dress up for eating. Camping, on the other hand, is relaxing, fun, and simple!

Pitch a Tent

When you're camping, your tent is your house. It keeps out the cold, rain, wind, dirt, sand, and all the creepy-crawly things. Tents also provide privacy and a sense of security. Even though it's just a layer of cloth between you and the great outdoors, you feel safer when you're zipped in for the night.

Not Tied Down
Freestanding tents stand without the aid of stakes and ropes. Once they're set up, you can pick them up, move them, and shake them to get dirt out.

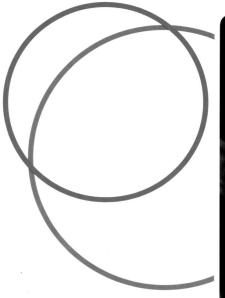

Tents are fairly easy to find. Pick one up at a garage sale, or borrow one from a friend. Outdoor specialty stores sell expensive, high-tech tents, and someday you may want to invest money in nicer equipment. For now, just use what is available.

The most important thing to consider is roominess. Make sure your tent is big enough to allow you and your camping buddies to stretch out in sleeping bags. You may also need space in there for your gear.

Make sure the zippers work. See whether the screens are in good repair. Check to see if there are holes in the floor that need to be repaired. Also make sure that none of the tent pieces are missing.

Then you're good to go!

Gear It Up!

Where you're going and what kind of camping you'll be doing are big parts of deciding what to pack. Camping at a state park is very different from heading into a wilderness area. Nonetheless, here's a list of the basics:

Tent: The most basic item is the tent, with poles to hold it up, stakes to hold it down, and tie-downs to pull out the sides. You'll also need a hammer to drive the stakes into the ground as well as to pull them back out. Don't forget a rain fly, which will protect the tent in wet weather.

Sleeping bag: Sleeping bags come in many designs. Some are thicker, for winter camping. Others are lighter, for summer camping. Most pack up nicely into a stuff sack for carrying.

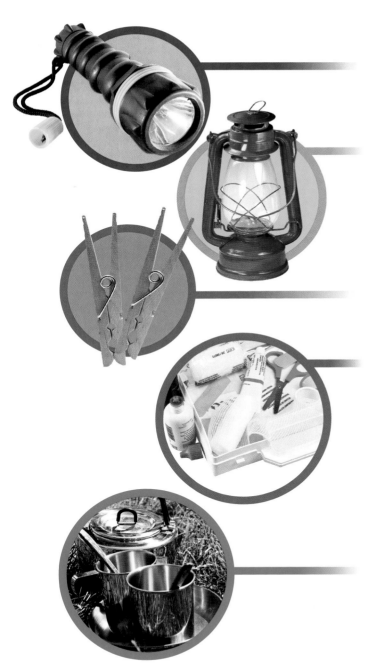

Lantern and flashlight: There are no light switches in a campground! Lanterns powered by battery or fuel will give you enough light to play some card games before bed. Everyone should have his or her own flashlight and extra batteries.

Rope and clothespins: Always bring a rope and clothespins. All sorts of things will need to be dried, including wet towels, swimsuits, and dishrags.

First aid: Don't forget the first-aid kit. While you're at it, better grab the bug spray and sunscreen. Bug spray will protect you from mosquitoes, ticks, and tiny flies called no-see-ums.

Kitchen supplies: A kitchen box will hold everything you need to prepare meals and clean up afterward: pots and pans, utensils, a cutting knife, dish soap, a can opener, and a container for hauling water. There are also the packed cooler and food boxes, but by the time you go home, those will probably be empty!

Critters You May Encounter

There are a fair number of critters with whom you'll be sharing your campsite. Some are as sweet as the birds that drop in to pick up your sandwich crumbs. Other animals are not so sweet. Follow some basic rules, and the animals you encounter will be the kind you can take pictures of, such as deer in the meadow or a raccoon washing his paws in the creek.

- Never feed a wild animal. Even a cute little chipmunk has a painful bite. Feeding

Up Close and Personal

Bring along a pair of binoculars and perhaps a field guide, a book to identify birds or flowers. If you're lucky, you'll see animals and birds in their wild habitat enjoying the great outdoors with you. Don't forget the camera!

wild animals is dangerous for you, and it's dangerous for them. Animals that are too used to humans and their food sometimes must be trapped or even killed when they get too friendly.

- If a wild animal comes toward you, back away slowly. Remember, most animals are as afraid of you as you are of them.

- If you're in bear country, make lots of noise as you hike through the woods. Sing, ring a bell, or talk loudly. Bears will get out of your way if they know you're coming.

- Keep your food safely stored and your garbage disposed of properly. Never leave a food box unattended. At night, food should be stored in the car or hung from a tree. Otherwise you may have a furry guest helping himself to your food while you sleep.

Leave No Trace

While you're in the woods, you're a visitor. When you visit a friend, you leave your friend's home looking just as you found it. You'd never trample down garden flowers, cut branches off trees, wash dishes in the bathroom sink, or carve your name on the kitchen wall at your friend's home.

All the same rules go for camping. Leave everything as you found it, or make it better by cleaning up after someone else.

"Leave No Trace" is an environmental ethic, a principle of right and wrong that is taught to those who love the outdoors. Leaving no trace is everyone's responsibility.

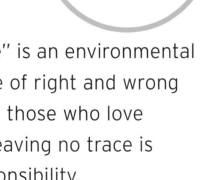

Always observe the commonsense rules of wilderness ethics:

- Carry out what you carry in. Leave only footprints.

- Don't damage living plants or trees.

- Take care of the campsite as if it were your own home.

- Don't use soap in rivers or lakes.

- Always use the outhouses or bathrooms. If you are camping in a wilderness area, make sure you always bury human waste.

- Use the fire pit for fires, or build one to contain your coals. Always make sure the fire is completely out when you leave the campsite.

- Don't disturb or take artifacts or other historical items.

- Don't disturb wildlife.

- Stay on all trails, and do not take shortcuts between trails. Walking off a trail can wear away the soil and destroy the trail.

Preparing for Mother Nature

Hot, cold, wet, dry—it could be any of these things when you're camping, and it might be all of them!

Pack clothes you can add or take off in layers, depending on the weather. A cotton T-shirt covered by a sweatshirt and a light, waterproof jacket is a good combination.

Even in the middle of summer, nights can be cool. Long underwear feels pretty good when you're sleeping on the ground. Long sleeves and long pants are good for protecting you from bugs and sun. Also make sure your clothes are durable.

Weatherproofing the tent is an important skill. Tent seams should be treated with seam sealer. Where the pieces of the tent fabric are sewn together, there are thousands of tiny needle holes that can leak. The sealer forms a watertight barrier as it dries. You'll need an adult for this job.

A ground tarp under the tent keeps rain and dew from seeping into your sleeping area. Make sure your tent has a rain fly, which is a tarp that fits over the tent itself. You may want to string up another plastic tarp overhead if you're expecting a hard rain.

A rain fly can keep you dry in wet weather.

Location, Location, Location

Here are a few important tips to keep in mind when you're choosing a campsite:

Are there a fire pit and picnic table? You can't cook in the tent, and it's awfully nice to have a place to sit down.

Make sure the site is big enough. Will you have room to pitch your tent? Will the tent be far enough away from the fire to be safe?

Have you ever heard the saying "high and dry?" It's a good thing to remember when you're looking for a place to put the tent. Place the tent on the highest ground, so that rain will flow away from it.

Is the tent area flat? Have you ever wondered what it would be like to sleep on a slope or roll in your sleep? You'll find out if you're not careful!

How far away is the water source? Most campgrounds have a pump or water faucet. But it's not fun to drag a heavy water container down a long path to your campsite.

The same goes for the bathrooms. You don't want to have to walk too far. On the other hand, you don't want to be too close.

Outhouses can be stinky. Flush toilets aren't so bad, but people use them at all hours of the day and night.

Check out the trees. Will they provide some shelter from wind? Will they give some shade in the heat of the day?

Safety First

There is nothing better than sitting around a fire at night while you roast marshmallows and tell stories. But before you build a fire, check with the National Forest Service, state park, or camping area you are visiting to make sure fires are allowed.

If you are allowed to make a fire, be sure an adult is around and knows what you are doing. Have a bucket of water or sand ready to put out the fire. Always use a fire pit.

1. Lay two pieces of dry kindling, or thin pieces of wood, together in a V shape. Inside the V shape, pile up some tinder, such as newspaper, pine needles, or dry twigs. Make the pile loose, so that air can circulate, but use enough to give the fire a good start.

2. Using small sticks, make a tepee of kindling over the tinder.

3. Light a wooden match, and tuck the flame into the center of the tinder. If it's windy, cup the flame with your hand. When the tinder

Collecting Firewood

Tinder is dry material, such as pine needles, pinecones, fallen bark, and dried weed tops.

Kindling is small pieces of wood, such as the dead branches of trees, fallen twigs, driftwood, or small logs.

Fuel wood is the big pieces of dead wood that help keep a fire going.

Remember to only collect fallen, dead branches for firewood. Never cut down or pull limbs, branches, or bark off live trees.

begins to burn, gently blow into the flames to help feed the fire. As your tepee catches fire, add bigger sticks.

4. When your fire is burning steadily, add a few pieces of fuel wood. But keep your fire small—a big fire can be dangerous.

The Outdoor Chef

Cooking while you camp is great fun. You'll be able to experiment with many kinds of foods and cooking methods. And you'll have a table full of hungry campers ready to eat almost anything!

Plan your meals, and do your shopping before you go camping. When you're camping, running into town for butter or bread can take a long time.

Most campers try to keep meals easy. Yogurt and cold cereal make a yummy breakfast. Peanut butter and jelly sandwiches are great for lunch. But it's nice to have a hearty, hot meal at the end of the day.

Everything just seems to taste so good when you're camping!

S'mores

You'll need: marshmallows
graham crackers
chocolate bars

1. Roast your marshmallow until it's golden brown.

2. Make a sandwich with graham crackers on the outside and the marshmallow and a piece of chocolate bar on the inside.

Corn on the Cob

Try baking your corn in the coals of the campfire. It gives the corn a delicious, smoky taste.

1. Gently peel back the corn husk, the outer covering. Pull out all the corn silk, the soft, stringy material between the corn and the husk. Close the husk again.

2. Soak the corn in water for an hour or so.

3. Place the corn at the edge of the fire's coals, and let it cook for about 15 minutes. Turn the cob over about halfway through the cooking time.

4. After it's cooled for a few minutes, poke the kernels to see whether they're soft. Add butter and salt, and enjoy!

Backyard Adventure

Right outside your back door, you'll find a great campsite. If your parents approve, you can set up camp in your yard and head inside if the weather gets bad. And there's no problem if you forget some supplies.

Set up camp and have friends sleep over. Pile into the tent, tell ghost stories, then sleep until the sun comes up.

You might get your parents or relatives to go backyard camping. Plan a cookout meal followed by some games, such as Frisbee golf. When it gets dark, turn out all the house lights so it's nice and dark. Lie around telling stories or singing songs.

You might be able to make a backyard campfire. Check ahead of time with the fire department to make sure it's OK. Or just use your barbecue grill to make hot dogs, s'mores, and burgers.

Sleeping Under the Stars

If the weather is warm and clear, try sleeping out under the stars. Watch the sky until you fall asleep. There are amazing things going on up there.

You may want to lie down on a tarp or thick groundsheet of some kind to keep the dampness away from you. Covering yourself with another tarp or groundsheet will keep the dew off of you in the morning.

Make sure your sleeping site is flat. It also should be smooth. Stones and tree roots are not good mattresses.

When you crawl into your sleeping bag, make sure you're wearing dry clothes—nothing that you were sweating in earlier in the day. Otherwise you're going to feel really chilled. Wear a hat to bed to keep your head warm and socks to keep your feet warm.

The Perseid Meteor Shower

Every year, from about July 23 to August 22, the Perseid meteor shower puts on quite a show. You may see more than a dozen shooting stars an hour. What a perfect time for sleeping under the stars!

We'll Be at the Campground!

State parks, national parks, private campgrounds—there are lots of camping areas to choose from, no matter where you live. Some people call this "car camping" because often times you can drive right up to your campsite.

Some campgrounds are almost like hotels. They have swimming pools, stores, and organized activities such as craft-making or hikes. Most, however, just have showers, toilets, and campsites.

The most common situation is a campground with marked campsites. You park your car right next to your site, pitch your tent, and start the fun. There's usually a picnic table and a fire pit.

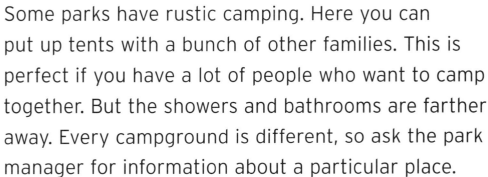

Some parks have rustic camping. Here you can put up tents with a bunch of other families. This is perfect if you have a lot of people who want to camp together. But the showers and bathrooms are farther away. Every campground is different, so ask the park manager for information about a particular place.

Before you pick your campground, ask your family members what they want to do. Hike? Fish? Bike? Swim? Canoe? With that information, you can decide which park is best for this trip and which might be better for a future trip.

Making a List and Checking It Twice

Camping checklists are easy to make. They keep you from saying, "Oops, we forgot that!" Write down everything you need to bring. Check off the item as it's placed in the gear pile or packed in the car. Some families use a computer to make the list. It can be printed for each trip and changed as needed.

Grab a Paddle!

Put your gear into a canoe, and head out onto the water for a few days. Make sure to wear a life jacket or other personal flotation device!

Some people explore lakes. Others float down a river. You paddle for a few hours every day, find a site to pitch the tent, and make camp for the night. Doesn't that sound awesome?

Canoe camping offers privacy. You probably won't have any neighboring campers making noise. You can enjoy the sights and sounds of nature, the peaceful darkness, and

the sunset over the water. It's just you and Mother Nature.

Many states have specially designated rivers with campsites for canoeists. Spend a few days fishing, floating, and camping on the river. You may pass by little towns, over small rapids, and through giant forests.

In northern Minnesota, the Boundary Waters Canoe Area Wilderness attracts thousands of canoe campers each summer. Hundreds of lakes connected by portages—trails over which you carry your gear and canoe—allow campers to explore large wilderness areas.

Call in the Experts

Consider making a trip with the aid of an outfitter, a professional who can do all the planning for you. Outfitters provide transportation, sleeping bags, tents, and all meals, and they might even offer you a hot shower when you return.

The Cool Thing to Do

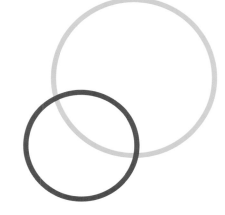

The Inuit people camp in winter all the time. It's no big deal for them. They've known how to stay warm and safe for thousands of years. But for the rest of us, winter camping takes some real skill and preparation.

Winter campers love their sport. There are no mosquitoes, and the bears are sleeping. It's quiet, amazingly beautiful, and challenging. A full moon on a winter night is very bright, and the silence of the cold is different from other kinds of quiet.

It's probably best to go winter camping with an experienced winter camper. That person can teach you how to dress properly, show you how to put up a tent in deep snow, and share tips on getting the proper equipment. Don't forget the snowshoes!

Snowshoes help you walk across snowy ground.

Cover Up

Winter campers know hats are important. A good deal of body heat is lost through the head. When the body becomes too cold, it will start shutting down blood flow, and therefore heat, to arms and legs in order to keep the core warm. Check out a balaclava, a cap that covers the nose, mouth, and neck.

A Presidential Camper

Born into a wealthy family on the East Coast, Theodore Roosevelt was fascinated by the outdoors. As a boy, he was often sick with asthma, a condition that sometimes causes difficulty breathing. He also had terrible eyesight. His father encouraged him to work with these challenges and sent his boy outside to explore the world. His father is quoted as saying to little Teddy, "You have the mind, but not the body. You must make the body!"

By the time he was 24 years old, Roosevelt was ready for a real

adventure. In 1883, he stepped off a train in Dakota Territory along the Little Missouri River and spent the next two weeks camping, exploring, and hunting. He so enjoyed his time there that he bought a small ranch called Chimney Butte.

Roosevelt soon returned to Chimney Butte. He traveled far and wide by horseback and camped on the open prairie or along the rugged bank of the Missouri River. He wrote several popular books. One of them was *Ranch Life and Hunting Trail*, which was illustrated by the famous American artist Frederic Remington.

When he became the 26th president in 1901, Roosevelt used his power to create many of the national parks and forests we enjoy today. He also established the U.S. Forest Service.

Theodore Roosevelt National Park in North Dakota honors this president. His cabin and ranch are visited by thousands of tourists each year.

An Island Adventure

Here is a camper's dream: a campsite right off a 1-mile (1.6-kilometer) stretch of white beach on a Caribbean island. You can spend your days snorkeling with the fish, windsurfing in the breeze, and hiking through tropical forests. Cinnamon Bay Beach in the U.S. Virgin Islands is a national-park campground on an unspoiled island with amazing sea life. There are tent sites, so you can bring your own gear, or you can rent a 10- by-14-foot (3- by-5-meter) canvas tent with a wood floor. There are also small cottages for noncampers.

Every tent is very close to the beach and comes with cots, a grill, a cook stove,

Cinnamon Bay Beach

a picnic table, and fresh sheets and pillows.

A camp store sells food and drinks, and a restaurant serves meals every day. There's also a water sports center that rents windsurfing sailboards, sea kayaks, and sailboats.

The national park also includes the waters off the beach, and the snorkeling is great. People report seeing sea turtles, moray eels, octopuses, nurse sharks, and big, colorful starfish.

And get this: The park rules state that campers can eat all of the coconuts they want!

Do-It-Yourself Tepee

Looking for more adventure in the back yard? Make a tepee!

1. Find a flat spot. Get several people to help you stand the tepee poles in a circle, tilting the poles toward one another at the top.

2. Using a stepladder, fasten the poles together at the top with rope or tape— or both. Make sure to have an adult help. The structure should feel sturdy.

Materials

- Four wood poles at least 6 feet (2 m) long
- Five old sheets
- Rope, tacks, masking tape or duct tape, and a staple gun
- Plastic sheets, such as a tarp or large garbage bags
- Old blankets and towels
- Screen or mesh
- Stepladder
- Markers or paint
- An adult

3. Wrap the sheets around the poles, holding them in place with tape, tacks, or staples. Work from the top to the bottom.

4. Make an entrance by overlapping two sheets to form a flap door.

5. Make a floor with the plastic sheets or tarp. Use old blankets and towels to cover the plastic and tuck around the edges.

6. Have an adult help you place some screen over the spot where the poles meet at the top. The screen will keep bugs away.

7. Be creative, and decorate the tepee with markers or paint.

On Top of the World

On the slopes of Mount Everest, climbers trying to reach the top of the world's tallest mountain spend weeks working their way up the mountainside. Each route to the top has a series of camps where climbers must stop to rest and get accustomed to the altitude.

The highest camps are at 27,000 feet (8,229 m)! Clouds pass below the campers. Many airliners fly lower than that. It's only safe to stay up there for a few days. After that, people can become sick from breathing less oxygen than usual.

Oxygen and Altitude

The atmospheric pressure, or pressure of the air, at the highest camps on Everest is about one-third that of sea-level pressure. That means there is only about one-third as much oxygen available to breathe as there would be at sea level.

The weather up there is rough as well. Horrible storms and high winds can keep climbers trapped in tents for days at a time. Temperatures dip to low levels, and frostbite is common.

Campers have all kinds of specialized gear, from mountain tents that can withstand 90-mile-per-hour (145-km) winds to camp stoves that are safe for cooking inside tents. Camping in the mountains with special equipment and oxygen is called mountaineering.

How's that for camping?

What Happened When?

1860	1870	1880	1890	1900	1910	1920

1861 Francis Fox Tuckett creates and tests the first sleeping bag.

1890 A Norwegian company begins selling the first factory-made sleeping bags.

1908 Thomas Hiram Holding, known as the father of recreational camping, writes *Camper's Handbook*.

1880s F.W. Linquist is granted a patent for a kerosene-fueled burner. This would be the predecessor to the modern camping stove.

1892 The Sierra Club is founded to explore, enjoy, and protect Earth's wild places.

1872 Yellowstone National Park opens, becoming the first national park in the United States.

NATIONAL PARK SERVICE

Department of the Interior

1916 The National Park Service is created on August 25.

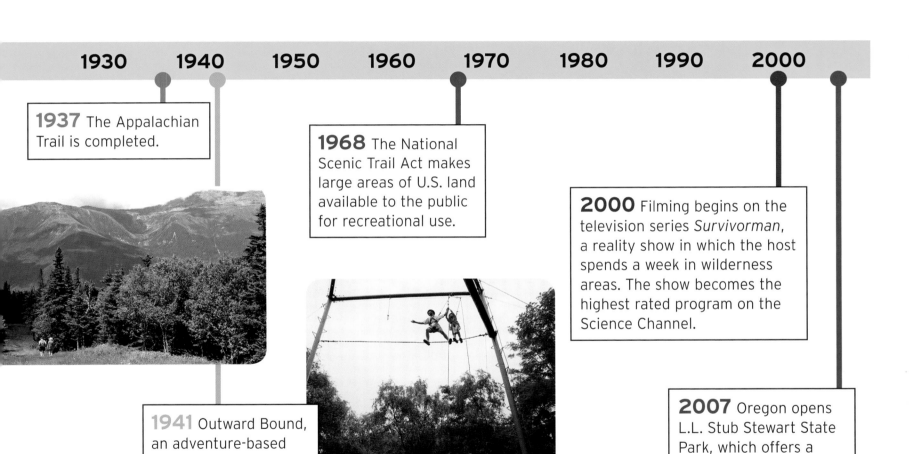

1930 **1940** **1950** **1960** **1970** **1980** **1990** **2000**

1937 The Appalachian Trail is completed.

1968 The National Scenic Trail Act makes large areas of U.S. land available to the public for recreational use.

2000 Filming begins on the television series *Survivorman*, a reality show in which the host spends a week in wilderness areas. The show becomes the highest rated program on the Science Channel.

1941 Outward Bound, an adventure-based outdoor education program, is founded in Great Britain.

2007 Oregon opens L.L. Stub Stewart State Park, which offers a place for people to camp with their horses.

Fun Camping Facts

Your body heat helps warm the air inside a tent. Body heat can raise a tent's temperature by as much as 10 degrees.

When you're camping, eat *gorp*, a word whose letters stand for "good old raisins and peanuts."

The Appalachian Trail is the longest marked hiking trail in the world, measuring 2,175 miles (3,500 km) long.

You can estimate the distance of lightning by watching, listening, and counting. When you see a bolt of lightning, begin counting seconds until you hear thunder. Each second is equal to 1/4 mile (0.4 km).

Chipmunks spend almost every minute during the day collecting seeds, acorns, mushrooms, berries, and insects. A chipmunk only weighs 2 to 4 ounces (55 to 110 grams), but it can carry its own body weight in food in its expandable cheeks.

There are more than 50 species of fireflies in North America, and each one has its own series of light flashes.

Small tents are called pup tents, because when they first came out, people said they weren't big enough for puppies to sleep in.

Mosquitoes are attracted to dark colors.

Camping Words to Know

backcountry: wilderness or park area away from roads and tourist spots

environmental ethic: the principle of right and wrong that is accepted by all who love the outdoors

ground tarp: waterproof canvas or laminated material that goes under a tent to help keep the tent dry

outfitter: a person who supplies all the necessary equipment for wilderness travel

rain fly: waterproof material that goes over a tent to protect against the elements

seam sealer: substance used on tent seams to prevent water leakage

s'mores: campfire dessert made of graham crackers, marshmallows, and chocolate

stakes: pointed posts that can be driven into the ground to help hold a tent in place

stuff sack: nylon bag in which a sleeping bag is stored

tie-downs: ropes that secure tents and keep them from blowing away; they also keep tent walls taut so they won't flap in the wind

ultralight tent: one- or two-person tent that weighs 5 pounds (2.3 kg) or less, designed for backpacking or portaging

Other Words to Know

balaclava: cap that tightly covers most of the head and neck, like a ski mask

habitat: the place and natural conditions where a plant or animal lives

kindling: thin, dry wood that is used to start a fire

no-see-ums: little bugs that bite, also known as midges; found near oceans, rivers, lakes, and swamps

portage: trail between lakes for carrying canoes, packs, and gear; it's also used for going around obstacles, such as waterfalls

tinder: small, dry material used to ignite kindling

Where to Learn More

MORE BOOKS TO READ

Drake, Jane, and Ann Love. *The Kids Campfire Book: Official Book of Campfire Fun.* Toronto: Kids Can Press, 2001.

Greenspan, Rick, and Hal Kahn. *The Leave-No-Crumbs Camping Cookbook: 150 Delightful, Delicious, and Darn-Near Foolproof Recipes from Two Top Wilderness Chefs.* North Adams, Mass.: Storey Publishing, 2004.

ON THE ROAD

Theodore Roosevelt National Park
P.O. Box 7
Medora, ND 58645-0007
701/623-4466

Yellowstone National Park
P.O. Box 168
Yellowstone National Park, WY
82190-0168
307/344-7381

ON THE WEB

For more information on this topic, use FactHound.

1. Go to *www.facthound.com*
2. Type in this book ID: 0756533996
3. Click on the *Fetch It* button.

FactHound will find the best Web sites for you.

INDEX

ABOUT THE AUTHOR

Jana Voelke Studelska is a writer who lives in northern Minnesota, where there are many forests and lakes to explore. She and her children go camping on an island in Lake Superior every summer.